LOVER'S ALLURE
BY
ALTONYA
WASHINGTON

LOVER'S ALLURE- A RAMSEY NOVEL
Copyright © 2009 by AlTonya Washington

ISBN: 978-0-982978115

This is a work of fiction. Characters, names, incidents, organizations and dialogue in this novel are either products of the author's imagination or are used fictitiously.

Printed in the USA by CreateSpace

A NOTE FROM THE AUTHOR

Hello,

      While reading this story, you may come across dialogue regarding events that have already occurred. Lover's Allure was crafted to take place along the same timeline as A Lover's Soul. So don't be alarmed, you haven't missed a thing.

Enjoy the romance,
Al

Lover's Allure

PROLOGUE

Near Invernesshire, Scotland

The wedding to unite Taurus Ramsey and Nile
Becquois, now Nile Becquois Ramsey, had been about as
exquisite an affair as any Kraven DeBurgh had ever
witnessed. It seemed the entire borough of Near
Invernesshire turned out for the gathering. The nuptials
were made even more special by the attendance of much of
Taurus's own family. Music and laughter mingled with
conversation and the subtle clink of glasses filled with
champagne or other spirits.

Kraven finally had some inkling as to how Taurus
must've felt when he was enfolded into the Near
Invernesshire clan. Though he and Fernando Ramsey went
back many years, Kraven himself felt as though he were

part of the Ramsey family who greeted him as if they'd all known each other for ages. It was no exaggeration to say Taurus and Nile's wedding reception felt more like a family reunion.

Still; as enjoyable as the festivities had been, Kraven found himself seeking the company of the one he'd seen far too little of. He and Darby had relatively no time to chat since she'd arrived the day before. Last minute preparations to assist her best friend the bride had the maid of honor running on one errand or another since she'd stepped off the plane in Edinburgh.

After stopping to speak or laugh over a joke with his neighbors or new found friends in the Ramsey brood, Kraven finally made it back to the manor house. He hadn't seen a trace of Darby outside and hoped to have better luck indoors.

The fact that he'd let out a sigh of relief the instant he saw her, didn't even register. All he knew was that she was still as incredible as she'd been when she'd disappeared in the car that carried her back to the airport, on to California and out of his life too soon after he'd first met her.

Leaning against the kitchen counter, Kraven folded his arms across the worsted fabric of the gray tux he'd worn as best man. His emerald stare was intent as it followed her pacing the opposite side of the room.

Cell phone in hand, she didn't appear to be the happiest camper while engaged in the conversation. Kraven felt for her but wouldn't complain as it offered him the chance to observe her unaware. The cream wrap dress was cut simple yet elegant in the way it draped her lovely figure. She hadn't looked his way once while they'd stood up for their friends. He; on the other hand, could scarcely pull his eyes away from her. So caught up was he in studying the enticing swell of her magnificent chest, that Taurus had to nudge him when Reverend O'Shay asked for the ring.

Now; standing there watching her with the intensity of an eagle surveying its prey, he had to ask himself just what the hell he thought he was doing. She lived in California for Christ's sake! Exactly how did he expect this- whatever *this* was, would work? He had no ready response to that question. He only knew that this time, he'd pull any string to get her to stay until he figured it out.

"Dammit Bebe, the girl's going on her honeymoon. Cut her some slack, will you?" Darby held the phone from her ear in order to sigh when Beatrice Woods, owner of the Wood Gallery in Oakland, CA continued to rant over the fact that Nile would miss the grand opening of her second gallery in Sacramento.

"Hell Beeb, has it been so long that you don't remember what a honeymoon is?" Darby tilted her head-squinting her gaze beyond the windows above the sink and hoping to catch a glimpse of Kraven DeBurgh. "Hell Bebe, would you rather be pleasured on a honeymoon or stand up in some gallery?" She snapped when a glimpse of Kraven wasn't forthcoming. "I mean, have you even *seen* the man she married? Trust me he's the only thing on her mind right now." Darby gave up on the window and turned. Her heart flew to her throat when she found Kraven there watching her. "Bebe, I'm hanging up now."

Kraven smirked and pushed off the counter. "Missing out on a lot of fun out there, you know?"

This time it was Darby who leaned as the mellow sounds of his deep Scottish brogue caressed her ears. She cleared her throat before she actually began to swoon over the man.

9

"Galleries wanting Nile for shows," she hefted the slim phone against her palm. "They've been right steady with everyone clamoring for an event with the newest Ramsey queen."

Kraven's steps drew to a halt when he stood a foot away and he relaxed before her against the kitchen island. "Good thing she has you to run interference for her, eh?"

Darby massaged her neck and missed the smoldering affect of Kraven's stare when it trailed the line of her throat and collarbone.

"Who's gonna run interference for *me* is what I wanna know." She moaned when the phone vibrated in her hand. Recognizing the name of yet another gallery, she cursed.

Kraven accepted the job and took the phone before Darby could answer. "She'll get back to you." He told the caller and pocketed the phone in his jacket.

Darby's laughter filled the kitchen.

"Now, I'm guessing you could use a break?" He closed a bit more of the distance between them. "You could always stay here."

Darby was speechless.

"No," she said once her vocal powers returned.

"Why not?" He tilted his head in challenge.

"My schedule-"

"You deserve as much of a break as Nile does, right?"

"We still have a gallery to run and the kids-"

"I've heard Nile rave over your staff-surely they can handle it all for a while. You may even build their confidence by trusting them to it, you know?"

Darby's lashes fluttered when she shook her head. Lord but the man had a persuasive voice. "I've got no clothes to last me beyond a few days."

10

Kraven shrugged and bowed his head. "We have a very lovely shop right here in the borough. The proprietor's quite proud of all the latest fashions she gets in from Edinburgh. Every woman loves to shop, doesn't she?"

"No where to stay," Darby whispered, slowly coming to the realization that she was fighting a losing battle. When an easy smile tugged the seductive curve of his mouth, she snapped to. "Don't *even* suggest it. I'm not staying with you-castle or not."

Grinning then, he dragged a hand through the lush onyx of his hair. "Manor house," he corrected. "And I was actually thinking of T's place right here."

"Oh."

"Well, well here you both are and discussing the same thing we were."

Darby trained her stare past Kraven's broad frame and saw Nile. She was leaning back against Taurus whose face held the same knowing expression as his wife's.

"I was just trying to convince Darby to take a few days for herself." Kraven innocently explained.

"And I think it's a great idea." Nile added.

Kraven played the role of the innocent. "I'm afraid Darby doesn't think so."

"Nonsense. She's been working way too hard." Nile argued, ignoring the slashing gesture Darby made with her finger across her throat when Kraven wasn't looking.

"So it's settled?" Taurus almost burst into laughter at Darby's wilting look which was in direct contrast to Kraven's gleeful one.

Darby only smiled weakly when Kraven turned, flashed her a cunning look and smoothed the back of his hand down her arm. Moments later, he'd left the kitchen with Taurus.

11

"Is there some rule against slapping a bride on her wedding day?" Darby asked when Nile sauntered close.

"Oh stop it, it's not so bad." Nile pressed a kiss to her best friend's cheek. "Actually, it's not bad at all. If you can't see how in awe that man is of you, you should have your eyes checked."

Darby waved a hand. "What are you guys thinking? You're on your honeymoon- I can't be hangin' around here."

Nile's expression dimmed for the first time in weeks. "I haven't said anything to Taurus yet," she glanced over her shoulder. "We won't be here long. I...I want to get back to my mother."

"Nile why-"

"She's my mother Darby, only one I know. She's going to need help-much help. Taurus won't like it, but I have to do something."

Darby was nodding. "I get it."

The light returned to Nile's eyes. "So it's settled, you'll stay? Kraven will show you the best time, yes?"

Darby felt swooning was dangerously close and nodded. "I don't doubt that for a second." She leaned into the crushing hug Nile gave.

ONE

Darby lay in her massive bed in Taurus's massive home and decided she'd have a massive headache by day's end. She'd go utterly nuts in the span of an hour roaming about that place and listening to her voice echo.

Lying there ensconced in cozy elegance, she cursed Nile and Taurus; who had left for Seattle two days prior. Just because they'd fallen in love there in Scotland didn't mean the same was in store for her- and with a man like Kraven DeBurgh? Who in the hell were they kidding?

A man like Kraven DeBurgh...She certainly didn't mean that in any way negative. Blowing a tumble of curls from her eyes, she conjured an image of the man. To say he was tall was an understatement, but he wore the breadth of his frame with ease. The leaning stance that he usually opted for made her think of some deadly animal at rest but still alert. His body was to die for and that went double for his face surrounded by the waves of all that lush black hair. The green eyes were deep set and made more vivid by the sleek midnight brows that slanted above.

Darby felt something tingle as the image grew clearer in her mind. Kraven DeBurgh was a man made to fall in love with and made to fall in other things with.

"Jesus Darby, stop it!" She hissed the order to herself, seconds before a booming sound had her shrieking and bolting upright in the middle of the bed. A second or two passed before the sound registered as a knock.

Whipping back covers, she rushed out and downstairs to find the man she'd been *conjuring* in her head, standing outside the front door.

"What's this? You're not up and about yet?" Kraven playfully chided, taking in the almond colored pajamas she sported.

Darby slapped her hands to her sides. "Up and about for what? To get dressed and roam around some empty mansion?"

"Ah…so the quiet's getting to you, eh?" He grinned and praised his ability to give her space for the last couple of days. His gaze settled on her pretty pink polished toes peeking out from the hem of her pajama pants. "I could help you out, but as you've already said no…"

Darby moved back when he ventured forward and headed down the main hall. "What do you mean?"

"Well…" he stopped in the den and leaned against the mantle. "There's plenty of room at my place, it being a *castle* and all." He grinned when Darby crossed her arms over her chest. "Besides, my staff could use the practice waiting on someone aside from myself." His gaze narrowed as he observed the unease creep onto her lovely face like a cloud. "If you're afraid I'd find my way into your room at some unseemly hour and do something unspeakable to you...well then, I could put you clear on the other side of my chamber."

Darby cleared her throat to hide the sound of the moan that chimed in response to the words. The *unseemly* throbbing which began someplace *unspeakable* would drive her crazy faster than the silence of that damned house. A few hours in *his* house and she was sure to be the one finding *her* way into *his* room.

"Seriously Darby," he strolled closer, hands hidden in the pockets of his loose fitting carpenter's jeans. "Nile and T would have my ass if I didn't do all that I could to make you comfortable."

Silently, Darby acknowledged that while the place was serene and gave her much needed time to breathe, she'd enjoy herself far more with others around. Absolute seclusion had never been her favorite thing.

"I haven't really slept well since Ny and Taurus left." She shrugged, "I'd hate to be rude to your staff."

Smiling then and pleased that she was softening, Kraven dropped one arm across her shoulders and led her back to the stairway. "Don't worry yourself over it," His head nudged hers when he spoke, "they need to learn how to deal with bitchy guests."

For the first time in two days, Darby's laughter lilted.

***

Kraven bypassed the castle and manor house and drove through the rich hills surrounding it all to a gazebo-like structure which was decked out for an elaborate breakfast.

"Did you plan all this?" Darby asked when she was able to make use of her voice.

Kraven shut down the Jeep's engine and seemed to be considering his response. "I may've laid it on a bit thick but I figured you're too sweet a lass to let all my hospitality go unrewarded." He nodded, satisfied by his reasoning then looked over and roused her laughter when he winked.

Darby studied the beauty spread out before her. "Is it so easy to get women to…reward your hospitality?" She looked at him when he remained silent.

"Would you mind my not answering that? I'm not sure you'd care for my response."

"Why?" Darby turned to face him in the seat. She was fully intrigued then. "Because it *is* easy?"

He grimaced, growing completely serious for the first time that morning. "It's pathetically easy. I've never had to work so hard to have a woman enjoy breakfast with me."

Darby nodded and turned back to study the view beyond the windows. "Is that why you went to all this trouble? The challenge?"

"You have no idea."

The stone intensity of his voice then had her studying him closely.

"But that you're a challenge to me isn't even a fraction of it."

Darby felt the smooth fabric of her mauve top begin to itch her skin amidst the heat inflaming it. "Tell me," she heard herself ask him.

The teasing light returned to his eyes as a devilish smirk emerged. "You're not ready to hear it, Ms. Ellis. Ah! Just in time."

Darby watched him leave the Jeep to come open her door. Breakfast had arrived.

16

Darby felt as nourished by the actual meal as she did by the conversation itself. Kraven's knowledge of food was incredible and she found herself literally hanging onto his every word. Not hard to do, considering everything from his face and body, voice and mannerisms were alluring to the point of holding her mesmerized. It was dangerous for a man to have so many enticing weapons at his disposal.

"Sorry," he mistook her set expression for one of boredom instead of intrigue. "Didn't mean to run away with the conversation. Have you had enough?" He waved toward her plate which only held traces of the omelet, toast and browns that had resided there.

"Stuffed," she groaned while pushing at the heavy plate. "I have to say that I honestly don't know how you store so much info about what mushroom tastes best with which spice."

For the second time that morning, an aura of seriousness shadowed Kraven's striking features. "One finds all sorts of things to brighten a day that's otherwise filled with truly depressing matters."

Darby fiddled with the delicate gold chain about her neck and thought she would've given anything to know what those depressing matters were. Nile had told her the man had a rather unsettling past, though one could look at him and see that. The scarred hands were powerful looking but possessed a surprising grace which she observed as he filled her plate with the delicious breakfast spread and her dainty teacup with some flavorful brew… She believed the man was a true paradox and would have loved to confirm her suspicions.

Of course she'd bet he'd be unwilling to share those matters that had once filled his days. What were they? And why did the easy humor leave his face when he spoke of them?

"Sorry again," he spoke softly as the devilish grin curved his mouth. "Didn't mean to get so serious there."

Darby pressed her lips together, stifling herself from begging him to tell her more.

"Guess it's time to get you into bed, then."

Oh, for heaven's sake, stop fluttering! Darby demanded of her lashes which set to batting the second he spoke the words.

Kraven chuckled at her reaction which helped to lighten the mood tremendously. Standing, he helped her from the table and back to the Jeep.

TWO

Darby felt like a new woman when she woke later that evening and it was no exaggeration. After two days of poor sleep, she didn't rise straight away but took time to savor the rugged luxury surrounding her.

Stone walls gave off a warmth thanks to the elaborate tapestries that decorated them. The windows were shielded by thick wine colored drapes that bathed the room in darkness-no matter the time of day.

Someone had been gracious enough to start a fire in the hearth. The flames cast a golden sheen upon the entire chamber. Like the walls, the stone floors were covered not by tapestries but with furs-dark and silken in their appearance.

Still drowsy, Darby snuggled deeper into the massive sleigh bed drenched in layer upon layer of heavy, exotically designed covers. The quilts looked to have been handmade and she wanted to doze back into oblivion.

Her stomach had other ideas, however. Darby heard the growl just as her lashes settled back down over her eyes. Perhaps a little coating of food, she decided. Then it was back to sinking beneath the covers for another lengthy snooze. Shoving back the thick quilting; she reached for her clothes lying on the armchair nearest the bed and pulled them back on over her under things. She'd misplaced the barrette which had been keeping her curls in a ponytail and out of her face. Shrugging, she tousled them about her face, sighed and pushed off the bed.

Darby figured she must've been conked out for quite a while. When she left the chamber, she could tell that it had grown darker despite the electric candles lighting the corridors. She stopped on a landing of the grand curving stairway, closed her eyes and tried to recall the route Kraven had taken when he led the way there hours earlier.

Sadly, she hadn't been paying the strictest attention to direction as they headed to her wing. God, but the man was a diversion and so unlike the well-mannered business types she was used to. Beyond the danger that seemed to shroud him, there was something elemental-more basic. This was a man who could change his civilized demeanor for a savage one like he might exchange one shirt for another.

So muddled was Darby in her thoughts, that she hadn't realized her nose had led her right to her dashing host. The aromas in the air were to cherish and called to her nose and empty stomach simultaneously.

Kraven was downstairs in what had to be the biggest kitchen she'd ever seen. There was even room for a small living area. He was dividing his time between

chopping something at the kitchen island and cursing at the gargantuan plasma screen which showed a hockey game in progress.

Darby pressed the back of her hand to her mouth in hopes of stifling her laughter when his team was penalized and he kicked a soccer ball across the floor. It bounced off the base of the sofa and rolled toward her.

"Ah," he whirled around and winced. "Sorry lass," he whispered, looking adorably sheepish as he did so.

Darby held onto the ball and moved deeper into the kitchen. "I never realized how loud L.A. was until I'd been given the chance to step back from it. Thanks for bullying me into staying a little longer."

"Me?" Kraven feigned offense while pressing a hand to his chest. "Nile and T did that, you know?" He grinned then as though he'd discovered how the gesture affected her.

"Do you like Italian?" He asked while turning back to the spacious kitchen island.

"Yeah, what's for dinner?" She took a seat at one of the barstools lining the island. She dropped the soccer ball while listening to him run down the menu. "What are you chopping?"

"Veggies for our salad. Had a feeling you'd be up by now."

Silence settled then with the exception of vegetables crushing beneath a knife.

"We're alone here in the house." He softly informed her, never looking up from the cutting block as he spoke. "Does that bother you?"

"Should it?" Darby was both surprised and pleased by the steel in her voice especially when her heart was beating like a bass drum. The look he slanted next could have easily melted the steel she'd celebrated mere seconds earlier.

"I didn't plan it this way."

"Of course you didn't."

Again, the grin appeared. "It just completely slipped my mind to tell you the staff isn't on twenty-four hours yet. Not 'til the lodge is fully operational, that is."

Darby reached for a baby carrot and chewed absently while he explained.

"I hope this won't prompt you to leave."

"Ha! No way am I givin' up that bed." Darby's reply was honest, but intended to keep things light.

Kraven flashed a wink. "I knew it'd be a good investment."

"So um, talk to me about this need to come back home to things that are more of your family's world." Darby was intent on moving the conversation towards anything that steered away from *bed*.

Kraven's chopping slowed. "What? Don't I strike you as a 'Shepard tending his fields' kind of guy?'"

"The truth?" Darby dragged her emerald stare from the bronze forearms beneath the raised sleeves of his navy sweatshirt.

His laughter rumbled throughout the kitchen. "I think you've just given it to me, love!" He chuckled a while longer, then reached up to swipe a laugh tear from his eye

22

as he sobered. "It's just what I told you before about the importance of finding one's roots."

Darby dropped the half eaten carrot and frowned. "I remember telling you that some roots are best left buried."

Kraven nodded his partial agreement. "You know it's often those buried roots where one finds his or her true calling." He dumped fresh chopped spinach leaves into a bowl. "Look at Nile for example. Do you think your friend would be such a champion for her kids were it not for what she knew of her own roots?"

Darby remained quiet, unable to argue the point.

Kraven sensed that and instantly regretted bringing the shadow to her face. "Hey?" He gave the island's counter a quick rap. "You just gonna sit there or are you gonna help me chop?"

"I was an army brat." Darby shared later in the den before the fire. Kraven had just asked whether she'd grown up in California. She was enjoying her second bowl of the amazing salad following a second helping of the delicious Gnocchi Di Spinaci he'd prepared.

"All that travel as an only child kept me from feeling too lonely. All the things I got to see and having my parents there to explain it all made me see the world as this great magical place, full of fascinating stories and wonder, blah, blah, blah…" She dug into the salad again.

Kraven waved the wine bottle in silent inquiry. "Why blah, blah?" He asked when she leaned over to have him refill her glass.

She drank deeply of the flavorful Riesling. "I was half way through middle school before I even had an idea about the complications my parents experienced because of their relationship." She wiggled her toes inside the thick socks covering her feet before tucking them beneath her on the arm chair and settling in for the story. "It wasn't until I had my own brush with racism that they said anything."

"Will you tell me?" Kraven asked.

Again, she drank deeply of the wine. "I was attending school in London," she shrugged to make light of the emotions swelling. "I didn't even know what the word meant that they called me." She smiled and looked down into her glass. "I remember going home and saying it at the dinner table. Daddy about had a fit." She laughed, happy she was able to do so. "My dad never went into all the specifics about the racial complications he and Mama went through but I knew they'd existed and I knew they'd been intense enough for them not to associate with family on either side." She tossed her head back. "Well my mother didn't have any family so...but dad...I knew he'd come from some big Irish *clan*," she smirked over the word.

"Anyway, my parents are all the family I have. Them and Nile. I never felt I missed out on anything and still..." she bumped the glass against her knee. "I can't get past that-that *morbid* curiosity to find out about that part of me-*my* roots." She sent Kraven a telling look and grimaced. "It terrifies me."

Kraven could see that without having to hear her speak of it. The dread of following through on something she felt compelled to do was scaring the living hell out of her even as an adult. His fists clenched on the arm of the worn brown leather chair he occupied. There was the powerful need inside him to cast away what vexed her. Somehow he suppressed the need.

"So how did your storm fear come about?" He half expected her to shy away from confiding.

"Hmph," she set aside the glass and shifted her position on the chair. "Nile thinks it's all about something from childhood-something in my subconscious, but I didn't develop it until the incident in London. I must've had a dream or something," her green stare was focused as she watched the flames dancing around the hearth. "I can never lock in on the details of the dream, but in it, I know I lose my parents. When I woke up, it was storming like crazy. The thunder..." she shivered beneath the fabric of her sweater. "I tore out of bed and through the house until I got to my parent's room." Leaning forward, she clenched all ten fingers through her curls. "I wouldn't tell them a thing I just huddled between them in the bed-shaking. I wouldn't let go of either of them 'til the storm ended." She blinked as if returning to the present. "We never spoke about that night and I never climbed in bed with them again but I hate like hell being alone when a storm comes around." She gave a jerky toss of her head. "If I'm alone, I try to focus the fear away. I haven't had much success with that."

Her attempt at a smile broke Kraven's heart. He had no choice but to go to her, hold her... He'd been trying like crazy to keep his hands off her, but wouldn't think of that then.

No words were needed, but he could tell she treasured the closeness. They both did.

THREE

Darby barely had her eyes open the next morning when the familiar booming knock sounded on the door. Slowly-*very* slowly she trudged from the bed to answer and found Kraven leaning against the opposite wall and checking his wristwatch.

"It's seven a.m., you know?"

"Seven a.m.?" Darby yawned. "Yeah…that sounds about right."

He chuckled and pushed off the wall. "So what are you doing still asleep when a day of adventure awaits us?"

"I can assure you, I've been having a very *relaxing* adventure right here in this fantastic bed and I'd be pleased to get back to it."

Kraven strolled into the room when she walked away leaving the door open. "And I had you pegged for a morning person."

Darby had to smile in spite of her drowsiness. "Not even on my best days." She flashed him a wicked look when his laughter seemed to shake the room.

Kraven prevented her from tugging up the covers when Darby climbed back into bed. "What are you wearing to the party tonight?"

"Party?" She queried through a yawn.

"Colin and Moira Bradenton's anniversary."

Darby nodded, smiling at the memory of the kind couple who cared for the manor house Taurus kept a few miles away. "I had no idea," she breathed, now sitting in the middle of the bed with her legs folded. "Nile'll sure hate she missed it." She said, recalling how sweet the couple had been to her friend when she visited.

"And you *can't* miss it." Kraven warned, his gaze lowering as he stepped closer to the bed. "Miss Moira already told me she had to have at least one of her girls there."

Darby felt her heart warm over the words, but fell back against the bed just the same. She tossed an arm across her head in a weary manner.

"What the hell would I wear to something like that?" She moaned.

Kraven leaned over her then, bracing a fist on either side of her against the bed. His deeply set jade eyes caressed her face before lowering to the wash-worn green T-shirt she'd slept in. The garment had been slowly driving him out of his mind since she opened the door and his curiosity raged with the need to glimpse what lay beneath it.

27

Darby wouldn't acknowledge that her heart was about to beat out of her chest. She worked to stifle her breathing, for she certainly didn't need to do anything more to draw attention to the endowments there.

"I have to say that your present attire is fetching enough but aside from me and the entire male pop of Near Invernesshire, it might night g'over too well."

"I'm sure of it," Darby smiled while rolling her eyes. "That still leaves me in a pickle then, doesn't it?"

"Not at all," he waved a hand before setting his fist back in place on the bed, "I know the perfect place."

"Really? Is it outside the country?"

Kraven's laughter rumbled but for a moment. "If you like." He was suddenly serious then.

Breathe, Darby had to remind herself. "Local," she cleared her throat. "Local is just fine with me."

"Well then, I've got the perfect place in mind but we'll have to hustle as Ms. Elena only keeps her shop open 'til mid-morn then she goes to work the brunch crowd at her husband's café."

Darby had to laugh over the charm of it all.

"So if you're done laughing," he leaned in and kissed the corner of her mouth when she nodded.

Stop fluttering, dammit! She ordered her lashes when he smiled down at her.

"You've got an hour," he said and was gone.

Alone, Darby rolled to her side, squeezed her thighs together and moaned into the nearest pillow.

***

Elena's Dress was as quaint as the lady herself. Tiny and dainty, Elena Wallace appeared almost giddy when she was charged with the task of dressing the best friend of Taurus Ramsey's wife. She chirped and bounced

28

around Darby for the better part of an hour and a half. Kraven wondered if Seamus Wallace might be wearing the hat of chef and hostess of his café that day.

Within two hours, Darby had a subtly sensual frock for the Bradenton's bash as well as a few other items to serve her for the duration of her stay. He watched her handle the bill and thought had anyone told him a few months ago that he'd soon be enjoying over two hours in a dress shop, he'd have figured them mad. What he dreaded now was that the time had passed so quickly.

"Thanks Mrs. Wallace." Darby was saying somewhat sheepishly as she took the two large white bags the woman brought around the porcelain counter.

Elena Wallace gestured with a quick shushing sound. "Think nothing of it, love. It was my pleasure."

Darby scarcely had a moment to hold onto the bags with Kraven standing right there waiting for her to hand them over. "I know you're screaming inside," she whispered near his ear.

"And whatever gave you that idea?"

Stunned, Darby looked around the purely feminine shop and asked that he do the same. "I'm betting you've never been inside a dress shop in your life."

The pretend offense clouding his face then only made him appear more devastating. "I'll have you know that I've had some of my most enjoyable moments inside dress shops."

"God," Darby closed her eyes. "I walked right into that one."

"I'll make it up. Are you hungry?"

"Starved. Since you wouldn't even let me have breakfast before we left. Some host *you* are."

Pulling open the lace curtained door of the shop, Kraven managed the bags in one hand and pressed the other to the small of Darby's back. "Come with me, then." Casting a devilish wink across his shoulder, Kraven called out to the little woman behind the counter. "Ms. Elena, we'll see you at Mr. Wallace's café!"

Elena Wallace waved off the couple after calling out another 'thank you' to Darby. She next grabbed the phone.

"Margret, dear?" She whispered once the connection was made. "Looks like our Kraven will be the next young and lovely thing to be taken off the market."

Following a simple yet delectable lunch of fish chowder, biscuits and ale, Kraven once again donned his cap of tour guide and treated Darby to an afternoon of sight seeing. This time he shared some of his truly favorite places which carried the two of them quite a bit farther than they had ventured during the previous trip with Taurus and Nile.

Like before however, Darby was in a state of sheer awe. She would've never dreamed she'd be standing on such revered and historic grounds. There was Loch Ness where she'd scrambled for her camera in hopes of snapping a shot of the famed monster. She inhaled the crisp, fragrant air surrounding Urquhart Castle-one of Scotland's most renowned glens that dated back to the twelfth century. By the time they got back to Kraven's there was scarecely two hours to prepare for the Bradenton's party.

"Will they be offended if we're fashionably late?" Darby asked when she rushed in through a back door ahead of Kraven.

Shutting the heavy door leading to the kitchen, Kraven dropped his keys to a dish on the counter. "Most folks 'round here are farmers-early risers," he sent her a meaningful look. "It's fair to say this thing may not run all that late."

"Right," Darby gave a quick nod and pulled her bulky sweater over her head. Fanning out the T-shirt she'd worn beneath it, she reached for the bags of clothes he'd brought in for her. A second or two passed before she noticed he wasn't moving to hand it to her.

Kraven was indeed struck. He'd spent much of the day trying to bore into his head the fact that they were friendly acquaintances through mutual friends and nothing more.

A load of swill? Sure, but it'd gotten him through the day. Now, standing there in his kitchen; watching her honey blonde curls bob and cascade about her very lovely face when she tugged away that damned sweater...

"Kraven?"

He snapped to that time with a wince. "Right," he handed her a bag then waved toward the back stairway where they ventured off to separate chambers.

***

The Baird Pub; the site for so many of the town's infrequent *gala* affairs, hosted the celebration of Colin and Moira Bradenton's forty-fourth anniversary.

"A few more events like this and we'll be the new Edinburgh, eh Lou?"

Lucas Morrisey, the pub's host, grinned while nodding his agreement with Kraven's prediction. "It's shaping up to be a fine evenin', fine evenin'." He said, patting his protruding belly made more prominent by the snug dinner jacket he sported for the occasion.

31

Lou wasted no time venturing around his host's podium to pull Darby's hand through the crook of his arm to lead her to a reserved table. Meanwhile, the pub's owners Reese and Margret Baird were mingling throughout the growing crowd. Guests spilled out onto the emerald back lawn of the establishment. The night was so pleasant-last minute changes were made to make the celebration an indoor/outdoor event.

Darby was amazed by how warmly she was greeted by the townspeople. She remarked to Kraven about it when they had a moment alone.

"It's no act." Kraven assured with a smile but didn't make eye contact when he spoke. "They're really intrigued."

"I can't imagine why." She laughed.

Kraven's broad shoulders rose in a slight shrug. "They're all wondering when they'll see my ring on your finger."

Darby's mouth fell open. There was no sound of course. She could only stare in disbelief, her vivid greens trailing the length of him in the oak jacket he wore with a coordinating crew sweater and trousers. Thankfully, he never looked her way, for she would have certainly wilted. Shortly, she was being hugged by Moira Bradenton who then pulled her off to mingle. It took some doing, but Darby gradually felt like her old self as the evening progressed.

Much later, she was alone and gazing out in serene wonder over the moonlit back landscape outside the pub. So much for farmer's hours, the place was still alive with music and laughter. She stiffened then, feeling her throat constrict when large scarred hands appeared on either side

32

of her along the brick fence. She ignored the chill that crept through the silk on satin coral fabric of the flaring wrap dress she wore. Biting her lip, she worked to conjure up a topic which steered clear of their previous conversation.

"So um, tell me about this fear of yours." She tried and heard his low chuckle in her ears.

"My own fault, really," Kraven began with the laughter still coloring his words. "Out and about along the outskirts of the manor house… I was runnin' away-got up early, packed clothes, food, set out…"

"Why were you running away?"

Behind Darby, Kraven shrugged. "Like every kid, I felt they didn't understand me. 'Course, I was only eight and it was for no reason as complex as that. Ma wouldn't let me go hunting with my Da and uncles that weekend." His expression sharpened, grown haunting in that moment. "Wasn't 'til I was about sixteen that the 'not understanding me' part kicked in and I made good on my threat to run."

Darby tilted her head when she heard the curse that followed.

"Worst mistake of my bleedin' life," he added.

Knowing there was a story there; Darby caught the chord in his deep voice that warned her not to probe.

"So the spiders were there to coax you back home at the tender age of eight?"

"Ah yes, the spiders," the infectious rumbling laugh returned. "I stumbled into a ditch, more like a well," he chuckled again and pressed a thumb to the corner of his eye to dry a tear. "The thing was filled with spiders, must've been thousands of 'em. By the time I'd run back home, most of 'em had fallen away."

Darby had to laugh as she imagined it. "I'm sorry."

"Not a problem, it *is* quite funny."

"No, no I *am* sorry." Darby shook her head. "You were kind enough not to laugh at me when I told you about my fear."

Kraven made her turn and face him then. "Yours is no laughing matter. Don't you ever make fun of it."

Her smile was shaky. "Thanks for not making me feel like I was completely screwed in the head when I told you about it." She let her gaze fall and focused on the weave of his sweater. "I've never told anyone because I knew they'd think I was crazy."

Kraven said nothing, only kept his hand curved about her neck while his thumb caressed her cheek.

Darby swallowed past the lump beginning to block her throat. She didn't trust herself to lift her stare to his but could almost feel his growing more intense. Her fingers tingled where they rested against his sweater. She pressed her lips together feeling his touch trail her cheek, across her jaw and to the pulse point thundering below her skin.

"Hey you two, Barrett Richards is about to give us a tune on the pipes!"

Darby expelled the breath she didn't realize she'd been holding. Lucas Morrisey's interruption was well received.

Without a word, Kraven offered his arm and they returned to the pub.

FOUR

For Darby, the next few days were delightfully non-dramatic and non-erotic for the most part. Of course, the attraction was most definitely simmering now between her and her dark mysterious host.

She'd never admit it aloud, but in her heart she knew she'd give the man whatever he asked for had he pressed the issue. At any rate, the days following the party had them sharing more about their pasts and their presents.

Kraven spoke mostly of his present and plans for his family's land. Darby knew he was trying to make them proud to make up for whatever upsets his past actions may've caused. They'd taken to having supper before the fire in the den every evening. There, the conversation flowed as freely as the wine that Kraven revealed came from a vineyard he owned in France. Darby teased that he was a true renaissance man and could tell he experienced a jolt of pride over the title.

One evening; after yet another incredible firelight meal, they were discussing that vineyard and various interests Kraven held.

"...I've been thinking of scouting some property out in California, but I've got a friend out there who owns a successful winery. I don't care for giving him the competition so I'm happy with the tutelage he offers from time to time."

Kraven smirked over the idea and then noticed that Darby wasn't responding. Leaning close, he studied her face and saw that she'd dozed off.

Smiling so intensely that his gaze narrowed, he smoothed his fingertips across her brow and tiny nose, and then toyed in the vibrant glossy curls that framed her face.

Falling for her, aren't you mate? A silent voice inquired.

Kraven winced. Hell, he'd already fallen for her...he knew she'd never believe him. He knew it would be because she'd be too afraid to. Shaking away heavy thoughts then, he stood and drained his wine glass.

With little effort, he reached down and tugged her prone form across his shoulder. With one hand clasped over her jean clad thighs, he used his free hand to grab their empty glasses which he deposited on the bar. From there, he took the stairwell that led from the den to her wing of the house.

He was shouldering open her bedroom door just as she began to stir. She'd awakened fully by the time he lay her down.

36

"You fell asleep on my winery story." He explained while taking a seat on the edge of the bed.

Her mouth curved down. "Sorry."

"Don't be. It gave me the chance to carry you." His eyes raked her in one sweeping motion. "I've been wondering what it'd feel like to hold you."

Unnerved and aroused beyond description, Darby glanced toward her ample bust line. "All this tends to fool people."

A helpless look mingled with the jade intensity of his gaze when he followed the path of her own. When the emerald orbs returned to hers, Darby realized it was no time to make remarks-teasing or otherwise- about her well endowed chest.

"Kraven?"

"Mmm hmm?" He replied milliseconds before his tongue thrust past her parted lips.

Shivers struck the length of her entire body and Darby moaned while opening her mouth to allow his tongue more room to explore.

His groan caught on a whimper as he kissed her raggedly. His hands were clenched in the bed coverings on either side of her while her hands tentatively spanned and then kneaded the granite slabs of muscle packing his chest.

She took note of her fingers curling into the fabric of the shirt hanging outside his jeans. She sought to bring him closer. She couldn't help it and didn't care. She wanted him so. Eagerly, her tongue dueled with his, her lips suckling his own before she kissed him all over again and reveled in the power she felt when his moans wavered.

Something snapped inside Kraven and he gave himself a mental kick for taking advantage of her. With some effort-*great* effort, he forced himself to back off.

"I'm sorry," his voice was barely a whisper. He couldn't ignore the disappointment on her face but wouldn't allow it to lure him back. He nudged her nose with his, kissed her cheek and dragged himself from the bed.

***

Sleep was a long time coming and morning arrived all too soon. As Kraven had done the night before, Darby dragged herself from the bed, ordered herself to dress and go downstairs. She certainly couldn't hide up there all day. Perhaps she could strike up conversation with the very hospitable staff and avoid talking to Kraven at all.

Such was not to be for she spotted not one of the efficient workers on her way downstairs-even when she arrived in the kitchen. No one was there...except Kraven.

In the midst of uncapping a carton of milk, he paused finding her there in the entryway. "There's breakfast," he cleared his throat and nodded toward the stove. "Porridge, toast, eggs..."

"Thanks," she whispered and set about fixing a plate. She did fine until his cologne drifted beneath her nose. The scent of pine and something else unfamiliar but all too alluring merged in through the aroma of the breakfast.

The dipping spoon she held fell to the stovetop with a clatter.

"I um, I'll take this upstairs." She said half glancing back at him before grabbing her food and hustling out of the kitchen.

The remainder of the day was a far cry from any of the others preceding it. The only real conversation occurred amidst the house staff who all wondered at the silence between their employer and his beautiful guest.

Darby passed on lunch, telling herself it was because she wanted to handle some business with the studio and maybe tour a little more of the castle. Kraven passed on lunch as well, deciding to catch up on work from his study.

By dusk, the staff had gone. That night's dinner was prepared and the two remaining souls inside the large house silently admitted they'd had enough of the distance.

As he'd done each night, Kraven brought dinner and silverware out to the den along with the meal they'd enjoy before the fire. At least, he *hoped* they'd enjoy it before the fire. He had no idea how to handle things now but thought if Darby would just come down for dinner he'd know where to go from there.

The smells of another succulent meal filled the air to mingle with that from the flame-filled hearth. Kraven barely acknowledged it. Hands settled deep into his khaki pockets, his gaze was narrowed to slits and pensive as he looked upon the fire.

Like her host, Darby had hoped they could enjoy supper in the den as usual. She'd paced her bed chamber for over half an hour before tugging a sweater over the snug tank she wore with faded jeans.

She was already down the back stairwell before she lost her nerve and decided to head back up. The exquisite meal however, tempted her nostrils and beckoned her feet to continue their trek to the den.

She bit her upper lip at the sight of him there before the fire. Flames danced across his extraordinary features, casting an element to his profile which was a cross between sinful and seductive.

Watching him standing there, head bowed, hands hidden in his pockets, leaning back on one leg while the other was shifted slightly forward as he stood on his bare feet...his allure called to her. It provoked her like some tangible entity. Her teeth threatened to draw blood from the lip she clenched and she whimpered when some unspeakable emotion caused her stomach to swirl.

Kraven caught the miniscule sound and his head tilted only slightly. Darby continued to watch him beneath the heavy fringe of her blondish brown lashes as she moved slowly off the last few steps and into the den.

Kraven set his jaw, his own lashes fluttering as the shameless desire for conquest shot through him like something fiery and driven.

Knowing she should say something, but having no idea what, Darby chose to focus on what promised to be a heavenly meal. She brushed past him on her way to the plates.

She never made it to the plates.

Without turning from the fireplace, Kraven reached back and caught a fistful of her sweater.

Some surprised, wanton sound lilted from Darby's throat but it never had the chance to reach full volume before being smothered by the force of his tongue deep in her mouth.

The kiss was as ragged as it had been the night before. The added intensity harbored on a dangerous determination. Darby knew she would have been more than a little unsettled had she not needed the intensity just as much...

FIVE

Kraven dragged the sweater from Darby's shoulders and she could hear him whispering something as her honey brown skin was bared to his brilliant gaze. After several mind-clouding moments, she realized he was speaking in another language. She didn't need it translated to know it was something smoothly, sweetly erotic.

Dinner was forgotten as he pulled her to the fur covered floor before the hearth. Darby felt shivers stab her body as if the blazing fire held no warmth. Her eyes were riveted on Kraven's darkly magnificent features. His eyes were riveted on the clothing he peeled from her body, first with his fingers and then with his teeth.

Her lilting cry returned when she felt him at the snap of her jeans.

"Kraven I-"

His hands stilled and Kraven conjured a silent prayer that he'd be able to stop if she should ask him to.

Darby licked her lips and rolled her eyes toward the ceiling. "I haven't been with anyone in a while-quite a while," she added and was terribly embarrassed by the fact as she always portrayed herself to be a woman with a healthy sex life.

The now familiar grin curved his mouth. "I'm glad because neither have I." He almost chuckled at her stunned expression. "I hope this means you won't notice that I'm terribly out of practice."

Laughter rumbled between them low and easy for only a few seconds then seriousness revisited the encounter. Without ceremony, Kraven jerked her out of the jeans and the lacy scrap of material serving as her panties. Only for a moment was she garbed in the snug white tank before he caught her wrist, tugged her up and pulled the cotton garment over her head.

Again, Kraven was captivated by the effect of the honey gold curls cascading around her face once he'd removed the top. As though a kiss would help him savor more of the affect, he leaned in to cup her face in his big hands.

Darby trembled when the tip of his tongue outlined the full curve of her mouth. Infrequently, his tongue delved in just slightly to graze her teeth. Darby's cry that time resembled a yearning moan she was so starved for his kiss.

Kraven was traveling the slope of her nose with his before teasing her jaw and the length of her neck. Darby reached out seeking his body still hidden beneath the black T-shirt that emphasized the sleek muscles of his biceps and forearms.

He didn't want her touching him-not yet. She'd bring an end to things all too soon as badly as he craved her.

Darby found her wrists trapped in his grasp while she was simultaneously being jerked into another kiss. Sitting without a stitch of clothing before a raging fire and being kissed senseless by a darkly gorgeous Scottish...lord was pretty much more than she could bear. She could feel the pressure building in her thighs and tore her mouth from his.

"I'm about to come all over your very expensive rug here," she warned.

His stare sharpened and the irresistible grin re-emerged. He insinuated a hand between her thighs. "Please do, I've got others." He brushed his thumb across her clit to help her along.

It didn't take much more beyond that and Darby was melting back onto the rug while giving into the orgasmic shudders that overwhelmed her.

Hissing a lurid curse below his breath, Kraven straddled her writhing form and bowed his head to dine on the full rounded perfections that were her breasts. Darby let her fingers get lost in the black wavy mass of his hair and arched to silently beckon his lips, teeth and tongue to a nipple. Her legs were restless and she tried to wrap them around his waist to bring him down.

He resisted.

"Please take off your clothes," she moaned, not caring that she had to beg.

"Christ, Darby," he almost sobbed wanting very much to lengthen the moment he'd fantasized about almost from the instant he met her.

Any more of her sensual invites and his fantasy would be fast forwarded. Far soon than he'd intended, he began to suckle a nipple hoping to fill her mouth with moans as opposed to words.

He treated the rigid peaks to a maddening array of manipulations. He used his lips and teeth to suckle and graze one nub while his thumb and forefinger tugged and squeezed the other. The fondling had Darby weakly beating her fists to his shoulders out of sheer arousal overload. Mercifully, he settled himself fully against her while hungrily bathing her nipples.

"Kraven...dammit, please..." her eyes widened as a stake of need lanced through her. He felt like pure heaven against her, but *inside* her was where she wanted him. Greedily, she clutched the fastening of his loose khakis.

When he grappled for her hand, she responded by slapping at his wrists. She continued to do so until he emerged the victor with *her* wrists again captive-this time one in each hand. He kept them pinned on either side of her body.

"Wait," he urged and then smiled when she pouted.

"I have," she argued.

"Wait please, please," he repeated the phrase while making his way down her body until his mouth rested at the joining of her thighs.

"Wait," he urged once more seconds before his tongue probed her wet, tight sex.

Darby realized she hadn't completely melted into the fur as her body now felt positively limp. While his tongue rotating and thrusting inside her were truly the things multiple orgasms were made of, they only heightened her desperation for a much stiffer and far lengthier part of his anatomy.

Deciding to make do with what she was being given, she began to ride his lunging tongue in hopes of finding her release. Kraven let go of her wrists to stay her hips, but she wouldn't allow it and simply drove against him with increased enthusiasm.

"Dammit to hell," he growled and rose to glare down into her passion drowsy face. "Hell," he growled again, kissing her while tugging her up from the rug.

"You're a torturer," she accused after suckling her taste from his tongue.

He held her high against him. "You have no idea. So stop rushing me, why don't you?"

They kissed madly as Kraven made his way out of the den. Darby whimpered when she saw he was taking the wide front staircase and received a slap to her bottom as payback for disagreeing with the longer route he'd chosen.

To *torture* her, Kraven stopped half way up the first flight, turned her toward the banister, bent her slightly and kissed his way down her back. He paid homage to the full swell of her buttocks. Then; taking one of her thighs in an unbreakable hold, he held her still for an intimate kiss from behind. His free hand snaked around and he used his middle finger to take her from the front. When she began to move up and down on the pleasuring digit, he of course ended the…torture.

Darby bit her lip on the cry she wanted to release. Never…no, that was correct. *Never* had she been taken so far to the edge. Never. And the man hadn't even removed a stitch of his clothing!

They were in the depths of another kiss when Kraven stopped again. This time just on the landing that led to his wing of the manor.

"No please," Darby cried out then, "I didn't say a thing," she whined when he turned her toward a tapestry covered wall.

God, but she was adorable, Kraven marveled knowing she was too much the way he'd have her. Still, there was so much he'd yet to learn about her. She had absolutely no idea how definitely her fate was sealed. She was his and after that night she was never getting rid of him.

"Kraven…Kraven, I-"

"Shh…patience Ms. Ellis," he crooned and scooped a fistful of curls, raking them up to expose her nape. He showered the area with kisses, his free hand moved round to weigh and massage a breast.

Darby reached up and around to fill her hands with his hair, but was once again overcome by the dull throb of need when his hand trailed from her chest. That time, his index and middle fingers filled her body. Before she could grind down, Kraven released her curls and used his hip to press her closer to the wall. One hand stilled her hip, while the other worked its magic at her center.

She had no pride no inhibitions left and sobbed being left with no choice but to take what he subjected her. While clawing at the tapestry, she cried into its crafted softness, in some pathetic effort to vent the frustrations of her raging desire.

When he finally pulled her from the wall, she had no fight left. When he stepped past the high arched doorway of his chamber, she was so overwrought she could scarcely appreciate the intimidating beauty of the room. With its dark, tapestry draped walls, fur covered floors and electric lighting the place was the epitome of exquisite erotic. The electric lighting cast the room in a soft golden

46

glow accentuated by the glow from yet another flaming hearth.

Kraven settled Darby to the middle of a bed that seemed way bigger than any king size she'd ever seen. She forbid her eyes to close upon realizing he was at long last disrobing. Like an eager child, she held the look of wonder while biting her thumbnail and scanning every square inch of muscled bronzed chest bared to her once he'd drawn the T-shirt over his head.

Just the sight of those hands going to the belt around his pants was enough to have her moan and begin a slow grind on the cashmere bed coverings. Like his hands, his body was covered with an array of scars. She found them more provocative than grizzly. Her gasp lilted to a cry that held a twinge of disbelief when his pants and boxers fell away revealing the extent of his erection.

Darby swallowed, eyes never straying from that part of him-not even when she moved up on her elbows to gain a...fuller view. Kraven smirked, but otherwise ignored her rather awed reaction to the sight of him. He turned to the table next to the bed and grabbed a handful of condoms from one of the drawers there.

Darby's head tilted in fascination as she watched him ease the protective covering down his shaft. When he knelt to the bed, she reflexively squeezed her legs together.

Kraven continued to ignore her reaction. Impressively endowed, he was acutely aware of his size...and hers. Arousing her; until she couldn't think straight had been a part of the plan but not the only part. The lengthy foreplay had also been to prepare her to take him.

Her mouth was dry with the need for him despite the fact that she'd never taken a man anywhere near his size before. Time to dwell on the fact though was useless when his hands folded behind her knees and he drew her toward him.

"Kraven," she barely had time to whisper his name before his tongue filled her mouth in unison with his sex filling hers. She cried out when just the slightest brush of discomfort nudged her.

Kraven's hold tightened. His drugging kisses gained potency as he sought to distract her-giving her time to get used to him. Unfortunately, nothing would take Darby's mind off the provocative organ that was presently filling her to overflow. The earlier discomfort had been so fleeting, she could have imagined it. She began to kiss him in wild abandon elation coming into play when she ground her hips against his and realized that time there would be no stopping. She could have laughed the sensations coursing through her then were just that devastating-*that* blissful.

Kraven felt weak and powerful at once and the feeling was more encompassing than anything he'd ever experienced. Ever. Breaking their kiss, he scooped up a bouncing breast and held it still for his mouth. He winced while suckling madly at the nipple. The sound of her cries in his ear had him shuddering in a mixture of satisfaction and arrogance over how he affected her. He could feel her coming against the sensitive sheet of the condom covering his shaft and pulled one of her legs from his waist to drape it across his shoulder.

The added penetration had Darby arching and letting her hands fall weakly above her head. Kraven willed himself not to come, knowing it'd be no great feat to be ready for her again instantly. He didn't want to stop. He wanted no lapse in time away from her. Her tiny breathless hiccupping cries were irresistible and stroked his ego and his cock simultaneously. Still grasping one of the honey brown breasts, he nuzzled his face into their hollow beneath her arm and tongue-kissed her there.

"Jesus Darby…" he turned his face into her cleavage and groaned, then gave into the demands of his body and joined her as she climaxed.

SIX

"Mmm…Lord DeBurgh…out of practice, my ass," Darby sighed, smiling her content when she awoke to the feel of his mouth roaming the dip of her spine and then upwards to her shoulders and the nape of her neck….

Lying next to her then, he smoothed curls from the side of her face. "Say that again."

Darby didn't misunderstand. "Lord DeBurgh," she purred that time.

He grinned. "How do you make it sound so good?"

Darby raised a shoulder and snuggled her head into the pillow. "I've got my ways." Her expression was pure wickedness.

He leaned in to capture her mouth in a sweet kiss that quickly took the road to lusty. "Say my name again... say it again."

Feverishly aroused once more; she'd lost count long ago; Darby delved her fingers in to silky black thickness of his hair and kissed him desperately. Soft, hiccupping sounds signifying her desire rose again when her sex tensed and puckered for him.

"Lord DeBurgh," she whispered in a half teasing, half wanton tone. Her movements were all passion though when she pushed him to his back and straddled his incredible frame.

Kraven kept hold of her hip with one hand while the other kneaded a thigh. Darby let her nails graze the heavy packs of muscle that made up his shoulders, arms and chest. In wonder, her jade stare followed the trail of her fingers. Absently, she wondered if there was even an ounce of fat on his body. It was cut sleek and hard like a living weapon. The comparison set her arousal thundering and when his thumb began to manipulate her core with torturous circular drives, she threw back her head and cried out in shameless need.

"Is it morning?" she was asking when she woke up next to the smells of food filling the still fire lit bed chamber.

Kraven was crossing the room. One hand held a platter teeming with delectables the other carried two heavy mugs which smelled suspiciously of coffee.

Darby reached for a mug like a needy child. She shivered when the aroma of the brew filled her nose. After a few sips, she set the mug aside and looked hungrily toward the platter he held.

51

Kraven took a butter slathered biscuit with intentions to feed her, but Darby reached for the platter instead. Boldly, she helped herself to hearty strips of beef bacon, scrambled eggs and seasoned potatoes.

"Bon appetite," Kraven teased while leaning back on the pillows lining the headboard.

"Are you eating?" Darby spared him a sideways glance.

He raised the biscuit and she shook her head. "Well I'm starved…I guess dinner went to waste, huh?"

"Had my mind on other things last night," he leaned over to nuzzle his face in her hair.

Helplessly, her gaze faltered to his lap. A soft yet still impressive penis rested against his thigh.

"I didn't like having to hurt you." He idly toyed with her curls as he spoke. "I know I can be difficult to take."

Darby smirked. "In what way?" she forked more potatoes into her mouth. Seconds later, she was laughing around a mouthful when he began to tickle her.

"Seriously though lass, are you okay?"

"At the risk of inflating what I assume to be a very large ego, I'll admit that I've never felt better." She watched him lower his head and marveled over the fact that he actually seemed embarrassed by her compliment.

"Well now…" he nodded then and sighed. "Now that we've got that settled."

Darby watched him leave the bed and go to the cart she hadn't noticed before. There, he prepared his own platter of food. Her mouth fell open. "You're kidding? *That's* why you weren't eating?"

Kraven sent her a blank stare. "What? We Scottish take our lovemaking very seriously."

"So you couldn't eat until I confirmed how good you were?"

Kraven shrugged, delighted to play out the tease. In truth, confirming that he'd brought her pleasure meant more to him than keeping up with Scottish lore. Still, he shrugged. "So to speak," he said and heaped on a mountain of bacon and potatoes. "Now I can focus on my stomach."

He turned with the platter in hand and Darby's mouth went dry at the sight of him erect and ready.

Kraven glanced below his waist. "Oh dear, guess I'll have to focus on my stomach later, eh?"

Darby fell into peals of laughter.

***

"Couldn't I have gotten dressed first?"

"Don't you ever venture outdoors naked?"

"In L.A.?"

"Forget I asked."

Darby had choked on what remained of her coffee when Kraven said he wanted to show her what all the fuss was about. When he grabbed a quilt and told her they were going for a ride, she was sure he'd been joking. Still, there was something...invigorating about trekking out on a still early morning, the land dew drenched and tinged with a heavy fog.

"Never been outdoors naked, never ridden on a horse..."

"Naked." Darby supplied and smiled when she heard him 'tsk, tsk'.

"These are things you'll need to enjoy more often, Ms. Ellis."

She couldn't resist shivering, loving the feel of his deep lilting voice as it vibrated against her back. The quilt did a more than adequate job of covering and warming them against the crisp morning air. An equally heavy pad rested beneath them. It covered the large leather saddle which draped the stunning gelding that carried them across Kraven's lands.

Once she'd gotten past the shock of venturing out in the buff, Darby's full attention was given to her surroundings. To say it was beautiful, breathtaking even, seemed so pathetic a manner to describing what lay before her eyes. Such awesome shades of green-vibrant and swaying when the wind kissed the high stalks of grass brushing the bottoms of her feet even from her lofty perch atop the magnificent horse.

"Easy Hadrian."

Darby noticed the animal's ears twitch in response to the cooing of its master's voice.

They stopped in the middle of a green sea. Rolling hills distanced off towards the glorious realm of mountains which seemed to promise a pathway to the heavens…Darby tried, but couldn't find words to express her amazement.

Weary almost from the utter incredibility of it all, she rested back more fully against Kraven's chest. He propped his chin atop her head and; for a time, sat silent as he too allowed the beauty to humble him as it always did.

"I spent over half my life running from this place. After a while, my family gave up on all their efforts to encourage me to stay."

"I can't imagine anyone wanting to run from this." Darby almost whispered.

Kraven shook his head. "Despite their kindness toward me, many of the townspeople are against my having a hunting lodge built here. They think I'm just trying to devise another way to feed my bloodlust while pitying my parents for not being blessed with more children."

She nudged her head against his cheek. "I can't believe that."

"That's because you know the man I am now." He kissed the top of her head. "Not the one I was. The one that's still in here somewhere...lurking," his hands flexed around the leather reigns he gripped. "The one I fear may make another showing sooner or later." He was thinking of his conversation with Hill Tesano then.

Darby heard the strain in his voice but knew she was still a ways off in prompting him to share his fears- the events that had shaped the man he'd been.

"Is the hunting lodge your only plan for the place?"

"More a means to an end, I- well..."

She nudged his abs with her elbow. "Tell me."

"You'll laugh. T did when I told him."

Darby shifted a bit on Hadrian and looked up at Kraven. "I promise I won't."

What he saw in her eyes convinced him. "I want to cultivate- farm it like my fathers before me."

She didn't laugh, though her lips did part in surprise. After all, no one could look at the man and believe him a humble, hardworking farmer. She didn't laugh though. She was too intrigued- too impressed to do that.

"Why don't you tell that to the people here? Try selling them on *that* intention?"

It was Kraven who laughed. "Love, they'd really think I was full of it then."

Darby was already shaking her head. "No, I believe they'd think you were changed, improved...matured beyond the boy trying to appease his bloodlust," she offered a lazy shrug. "They'd never see it coming and might just be curious enough to see if you could pull it off."

"That's not bad, you know?" Kraven's long onyx brows raised a tad above his deep eyes as if he were seriously considering her opinion.

Again, Darby shrugged. "It's what I do- Getting people to realize their marketing potential. I'm pretty good at it." Smiling curiously then, she scanned the view with renewed intensity. "All this property of yours…larger than some towns I've driven through. Are you prepared for all the work involved?"

Silently, Kraven mused that the work itself was the driving force behind him wanting to do it. His grandfather had once said he could lose himself in working the land. All his preoccupations, all his nightmares vanished like morning dew during a good toil in the land. His grandfather's sentiment had called to him more and more as he'd aged.

"Kraven?"

"I expect I'll hire out half the town," he explained after tuning back into their conversation. "Maybe even the next three or four villages and boroughs. But I suspect I'll be able to cut back once my sons are old enough."

She tensed so slightly, it might have been imagined. Kraven felt it easily enough.

"So…you want kids?"

"As many as my wife will let me plant inside her," He spoke the words close to her ear.

Darby swallowed. "I see…*lots* of kids."

"You think that's unrealistic."

She tried to dismiss the discomfort swelling her throat. "It's um…it's different these days. So many challenges…so much ugliness in the world."

"That's what family and strong parents are for, right? Giving a good foundation, morals…"

56

"Well didn't your parents provide that very thing? And still-"

"Still I ventured off into a life of *uneasy* business." He thought of Moira Bradenton's preferred manner of describing his past exploits. "I ventured off, but I returned unable to deny what I'd been raised to honor- to carry on."

"I wish you luck then," Darby's voice stiffened as she'd had enough of the conversation.

Kraven took her by the chin and made her face him. "Do you? Do you really?"

Her green eyes narrowed toward his. "Well...yes, yes sure I do."

"Enough to help me make it happen one day?"

Darby laughed though the gesture held no real steam. "What?"

"You heard me."

"I don't- I don't understand."

"I think you do."

"You're insane."

"I've been called worse."

She turned and bowed her head. "You don't know what you're saying."

Kraven cocked his head. "Very sure of yourself, aren't you?"

"You don't know me."

"And you don't know me."

"And this makes sense to you?"

He laughed. "Not at all, it's altogether irrational which is why I trust it."

She whipped her head round to glare up at him. "You really are insane."

His wink was devilment personified. "Starting to second guess your decision to stay with me here?"

He kissed her before she could answer. When he finally let her up for air, she could hardly recall her question.

"Well?" He probed.

"Uh...no," she admired her ability to form the weak response.

"Hmm...no, I don't think I'm convinced. What about you, Hade?" He called to the animal whose ears twitched eagerly. "Let's say we do more to convince her."

Darby found her mouth occupied again before she could question his intentions. Very impressively; and without once breaking their kiss, Kraven turned her to face him in the saddle they shared. He took the reigns in one hand while gripping her hips to settled her astride him.

Darby broke the kiss and pressed softly against the broad plane of his shoulders. "Kraven-"

"Trust me," he whispered, scraping his perfect teeth down her throat while settling her onto his arousal.

The moan in her throat sounded like something both elated and lamenting. Would she ever find another man who could turn her into a woman so weakened by the sheer thought of his body inside hers?

Faintly, she could hear her name on his lips. When she completely covered his shaft, he began to lift and rotate her. He orchestrated her movements as her nails curved limply into his chest. Arousal was mesmerizing her. Gone were the inhibitions that had her unnerved about taking and being taken outside the privacy of his bedroom. All that mattered was the power in his grip as he moved her to his satisfaction.

Mingled with her gasping cries were the subtle slaps of their bodies moving in sync to a seductive rhythm only they could feel. As if he were her lifeline, Darby hooked an arm tightly around his neck. Her free hand cupped his jaw and she kissed him languidly. Kraven; in turn, squeezed her hips, slowing their movements to keep time with the thrusts of her tongue against his.

As he'd done earlier, Darby raked her teeth down his throat. Her tongue darted out to test the unyielding chords lining his neck. Kraven buried his face in her hair and inhaled the floral scent of her honey curls while her mouth moved along the base of his throat, collarbone and further across his chest. He was overwrought by the sensation of feeling the slick snugness of her sex without barriers. Her mouth glided upwards once more and she nuzzled the dip beneath his ear before fastening her teeth to the lobe and gnawing it softly. There was the barest hint of possessiveness in the act.

Kraven reciprocated, dipping his head to her shoulder and sinking his teeth to the silken brown skin that beckoned him to taste and relish its sweetness. Glancing across her shoulder, he tugged Hadrian's reigns and clicked his teeth in the meaningful manner that instructed the animal to move on.

Darby's gnawing on his ear came to an abrupt halt and Kraven's smile was knowingly arrogant. Her moan that time, resembled a sob when Hadrian's slow gait shifted his body and in turn theirs, invoking sensations as indescribable as the land they stood in the midst of.

"What...what are you doing?" She sobbed feeling as though her hips moved of their own accord in Kraven's weakened embrace.

"Hadrian's walking affects us, love." He murmured, wincing at the delicious clutch and release of her sex around his. He clicked his teeth again and Hadrian's gait gained just a slight increase in speed.

"Kraven please…mmm…"

"You want him to stop?"

"God no," she pounded a fist to his chest while increasing the speed of her own movements.

Kraven assumed control again. Capturing her waist, he manipulated her. The dips and sways beneath their bodies as Hadrian trotted, had Darby climaxing in record time.

Kraven wasn't about to let the moment end and he continued to pummel her with more intense thrusts. The quilt draping their hips provided a provocative shield against the uninhibited coupling taking place beneath it.

Darby threw back her head, unconsciously offering her full bosom to his hungry mouth. Kraven accepted and feasted eagerly. One hand held a mound in place to be suckled mercilessly, the other clutched her thigh in a vice grip. He subjected her to both increased penetration and a unique rotation from his thick shaft as the horse continued its stroll.

"Darby…" he groaned on a helpless whine when she came heavily, drenching his sex and the covering they bounced on. His need soon mingled there with hers.

Hadrian's prancing slowed almost in unison with Kraven's and Darby's breathing. When Hadrian's stroll brought them back to the manor house, they were both spent and knew it'd be a chore sliding from the animal's back.

Kraven's strength was commendable though. He led Hadrian up a hilly path through heavy brush and trees until they came up on one side of the house. Keeping the quilt tucked round them and Darby in his arms, Kraven slid down. He took a short brick stairway up to a wooden door which opened to another stairway that provided a private entrance to his bedchamber. He was shouldering open the door, when he caught the teasing glint in Darby's emerald stare. His own emerald gaze sparkled and he smirked in spite of himself.

"Man's gotta be prepared." He explained and his deep laughter mingled with her chuckles.

SEVEN

"Why can't things run this smooth when we're there?" Darby demanded playfully of office manager Shelby Moss.

Shelby let loose a secretive laugh through the phone line. "You and Nile just don't have my skills."

"Clearly," Darby stretched her legs along the window seat where she sat studying the view from the rear of the manor house. "Seriously, are you really doing okay back there?"

"I'm really doing okay."

"And our new acquisitions? They still having the desired effect?"

"You bet they are." Another laugh colored Shelby's words. "Folks are really taking an interest in them and the five dollar admission fees we're charging are providing an impressive stash of mad money for the kids."

"Oh Lord, Shelby please don't let 'em get too crazy."

"Please, you and Nile would be so surprised and proud. The older ones are really getting an education on running a business- they're being absolutely frugal with that money."

The blondish brown line of Darby's brows raised several notches. "The teenagers?"

"The teenagers," Shelby confirmed. "A few people have stopped in to ask about buying some of the pieces, but the kids decided they'd make more money keeping the work in house."

"And um, what about my painting?" Darby bit her lip while inquiring of the piece she'd taken a special liking to.

"It's safe and sound."

Darby relaxed a bit, thinking of the woman who'd donated the work she'd fallen in love with. "You took it to my place?"

"Just like you asked. I even found a nice wall for it in that little alcove off from your den."

Darby brightened at the thought and hugged herself. She imagined enjoying the hauntingly lovely piece and a fragrant mug of tea in her favorite area of her condo.

"Can't wait to see it," she said as if talking to herself. "Shelby thanks so much for taking such good care of things while we're away."

"You bet. You keep having a good time, alright?"

"You bet." Darby reciprocated then shared another quick laugh with Shelby before the call ended.

Kraven waited until Darby put away her cell before he moved deeper into the room. He'd be blind not to see how much she was missing home and knew she'd be wanting to go soon. His frustration surged for a fleeting instant at the thought.

He didn't want her to go, had even toyed with the idea of locking her in the tower…He smiled and shook his head. Although the sex was supreme, he knew it wouldn't keep her there. He wouldn't want it to. They couldn't hide and; there in the serenity of his home, was what they'd been doing. He cleared his throat then and uttered an apology when she whirled around as though startled.

"I know you'll be thinking of leaving soon and I wanted to show you Edinburgh."

"Edinburgh." Darby whispered and looked back out the window. "I've only seen a bit of it during my two plane trips."

"I think you'll like it." He eased his hands into his pockets and leaned against the wall. "Faster paced than what we've got here." He glanced toward his bare feet and more softly said, "I keep a place there I think you'd like to see."

Darby dragged her gaze from the green hills. "More incredible than all this?"

His stare never left her face. "Nothing's more incredible than all this."

"When would we leave?" She forced herself not to ask exactly what he was referring to. Especially when she already knew.

"I'll let you know." He looked away before she could glimpse his jaw tightening.

Silence settled and the air seemed weighted by the tension. The mood seemed to encourage Darby to venture toward the conversation she'd been avoiding.

Kraven suddenly pushed off the wall. "I'll let you know about the trip."

He left as quickly as he'd appeared. Darby brushed a hand across her high ponytail and ordered her nerves to calm. Unfortunately, she knew what she had to tell him would do nothing but make things tenser than they had unexpectedly become.

She thought back to the things he'd said to her that morning with Hadrian... As beautiful as they were, it could never happen. He had to see that. Of course, it'd be hard to see anything ensconced in fairy land and falling faster everyday.

Edinburgh. Yes, Edinburgh was the place. Faster paced-more her cup of tea. She'd be more herself, more able to bit the bullet and tell him this had to end.

A nice, long distance friendship was all it could ever be- all it ever need be.

***

Edinburgh, Scotland~

Two days following Kraven's decision to show Darby a faster pace in Scotland, he was making good on his promise.

Edinburgh was as awesome as everything Darby had already seen. With the added, worldly allure of its magnificent buildings and breath-stealing skylines it was as though a bit of Darby's home turf had mingled within the historic beauty of the city. More than once, she had to remind herself to shut her mouth. It couldn't be helped of course as her eyes feasted on one incredible sight after another.

Kraven figured a drive; as opposed to flying, would be more enjoyable for a sight seeing trip. As one can practically drive anywhere in Scotland in a day, the two set out before dawn for the trip.

A smile permanently camped out upon Kraven's mouth since Darby had spotted the first of numerous sights early that morning. He was thrilled that his idea had met with such success. He grinned a little more whenever her hushed sounds of wonder gained just a bit more volume.

Darby was rather subdued though when Kraven turned into a wide stone drive that led the way to a towering construction at the very end of a long path. Elements of the old world and new seemed to collide in a provocative mesh of understated loveliness and vibrant magnificence.

Kraven left the Rover idling and stepped out to meet the valet who rushed over to greet him. Following a brief conversation, Kraven walked over to collect Darby from the passenger side.

"Wow," was all she could manage while smoothing her hands across the black cotton of the long sleeved hoody she sported with matching Yoga pants.

This was five-star living at its best, she mused as they headed toward the Muir Inn. Kraven escorted her across the beige and crème checkerboard floor, decorated with mahogany suede round sofas. The front desk area appeared to circumference the lobby in a rich construction of glossy oak that emphasized the subtle elegance of the flooring and furniture.

"Don't we need to check in?" Darby's fingers tightened into the sleeve of the white sweatshirt he wore beneath a Dolphins throw-back jersey.

"No need," Kraven tilted his head up to those behind the front desk who recognized him. "I keep a place here, remember?"

"Right," she whispered just as the echo of their footsteps silenced upon heavy chestnut carpeting covering the elevator bay.

"Our bags," she recalled as the oak elevator doors shut.

The look Kraven slanted sent her nodding again. "Taken care of," she said knowing he must be thinking she was completely unused to the 'good life'. While month long castle stays and weekends in five star hotels weren't the norm for her, she wasn't completely without couth. What was beginning as a time to treasure wouldn't pass without them having a very serious and perhaps unpleasant conversation.

Thoughts of confrontations and upset fled Darby's mind once Kraven unlocked a set of double doors and waved her past the threshold.

"Unbelievable," she said gazing up wide eyed and open mouthed.

The split level suite was furnished in an elegant burgundy and navy color scheme, with rich hunter green streaking through out. The lower level was completely old world design with a roll top desk in one corner, stern yet comfy looking armchairs off-setting a claw foot oak table and hand-carved fireplace.

The fireplace was already ablaze with a welcoming flame in the living room arranged before another set of double doors. A fabulous view of the quaint area waited beyond the glass. Dual stairways led the way to the level which was fashioned in a much more contemporary style. At first glance, Darby saw that it offered more of a view of the city. She could hardly wait to see the area lit against the night skies.

Waiting however, was just what she'd have to do, for no sooner had she stepped out to the balcony, Kraven was behind her. He encircled her in a snug embrace and pressed a kiss to her head.

"So you've got two choices. I can have you now and you can have your tour later or," he paused to nuzzle her ear while a hand slipped beneath the hem of her jersey top, "you can have your tour now and I can have you later. I'm partial to the first choice," he added for good measure.

"Hmm…" she pretended to consider it. "But you've forgotten about choice number three." She turned, standing on her toes to rest her face in the crook of his neck and inhale his scent. "You can have me now *and* later and we can just work in the tour another time."

The captivating grin appeared and he cupped her chin. "Why Ms. Ellis, the things you say." His voice lilted seconds before he took her mouth.

***

While the tour could wait, eating could not. Following several enjoyable hours *touring* the rooms in his suite, Kraven suggested dinner at the Inn's bistro. The suggestion was made in part because the food was unmatched and because he knew where his thoughts would remain if they didn't venture out.

That fact hit home when he saw Darby coming downstairs. The long-sleeved black frock would have been simple enough were it not for the oval cut in the bodice that gave a teasing view of the twin honey swells of her bosom.

He rolled his eyes away and pretended to be at war with the cuffs of the gray shirt peeking out from the sleeves of his black suit coat.

The desk phone rang and Darby decided to head on out while Kraven handled the call. He studied the sway of her hips and the way the flaring hemline and spaghetti strapped heels accentuated her legs. He managed to answer the call before it went to voicemail.

There were few places where the corridors rivaled the lodgings for loveliness but the Muir Inn's corridors boasted precisely that. The same rich chestnut carpeting ran throughout and the walls were lined with elaborate oil paintings that kept Darby occupied by their abstract qualities.

While waiting there for Kraven, she moved on down the hall to stare at the streets. The area had grown quite busier with the onset of the evening activities which drew people in droves. Darby was absorbed with the view from the floor to ceiling window at the end of the hall. It took some time before she noticed the handsome heavy set man who watched her from his spot outside the door of Kraven's suite.

The man was simply staring. Regardless, Darby's temper began a slow simmer. Kraven had finished his call and was just stepping out into the corridor when he noticed her being approached. He assumed a leaning stance against his door and waited.

"Do you know how lovely you are?"

Darby blinked at the man's question. She'd expected a remark but not quite that one.

"You canna possibly be here alone?" He continued.

She tilted her head. "Any why is that?"

The man chuckled. "Lass, no woman who looks the way you do remains alone in Scotland for long."

"Maybe I'd like to be alone."

"Understood," he nodded, "but should you change your mind-"

"I won't."

Kraven cleared his throat then, smiling when he captured their attention.

The man speaking with Darby appeared more than a little relieved by the interruption.

"Cullen," Kraven greeted when the man reluctantly left Darby's side.

Cullen Nevis clasped one of Kraven's hands between both of his beefy ones. "Heard you were around, thought I might stop up for a drink." He looked Darby's way. "Understandably, I got a little side-tracked."

"Understandably," Kraven's lips twitched as he fought to suppress laughter. He took Cullen's arm and drew him down the hall.

"Cullen Nevis, Darby Ellis."

Cullen's expression brightened as his blue eyes twinkled. "Ah...so she's yours." He clapped Kraven's shoulder. "I might've known." Clearing his throat, he extended a hand for shaking. "Ms. Ellis," he greeted.

"I'm mine, Mr. Nevis." Darby clarified while accepting the shake. "Nice to meet you," She walked on, leaving both men staring after her.

"God man," Cullen breathed, "where in creation did you find her?"

Kraven bumped Cullen's shoulder with his own. "She found me. She found me." He said and followed Darby to the elevators.

EIGHT

"People in Scotland can't possibly eat dinner like this every night and live past forty." Darby marveled later while studying her menu.

Kraven shrugged, frowning slightly as he too studied the bistro's choices. "We're a nation of hearty eaters. It's in our blood."

"I'll say," Darby laughed as she spotted a dish called Cauliflower Cheese and Whiskey.

The couple was still scanning menus when Kraven's name was called and yet another acquaintance stopped to chat.

Chatting however was clearly a ruse to take a closer look at Kraven DeBurgh's dinner companion.

Erik McHale greeted his old friend absently. His vivid blue gaze was riveted on Darby. He reached for her

71

hand and introduced himself after only a few seconds of conversation with Kraven.

"Erik McHale, Ms. Darby Ellis of California." Kraven shared.

Erik's thin face revealed deeper interest. "California... well you're a beauty- an absolute beauty."

Darby coolly extracted her hand from his. "It's a pleasure to meet you."

"No love, the pleasure is most definitely mine." He smiled and then turned to knock a fist to Kraven's shoulder. "Nice DeBurgh, very nice."

Kraven barely nodded and never looked away from Darby. "Are you ready to order?" He asked once they were alone.

She pushed her menu across the table. "Whatever you're having is fine with me."

Kraven waved and within seconds a waiter arrived. As the evening continued, Kraven settled in to observe Darby more closely than usual. He was most intrigued by the way she accepted the compliments that continued from his many acquaintances that approached the table. When they were half way through the meal, Kraven decided to prove to himself that he wasn't imagining things.

"Do you have any idea how incredible you are?" he leaned across the table and asked her.

She bristled, the knife and fork she held paused over the honey and lemon chicken. "If I didn't know it before tonight, I do now."

Kraven barely smirked. Dinner passed in silence.

The silence went on and could have probably gone on through the night when they returned to the suite. Darby strolled over to gaze out from the lower level balcony while

Kraven dropped his keys to the message desk. He followed her across the room, hands hidden in his pockets.

"So how'd you enjoy your meal?" He bowed his head to ask. "'Spose it was pretty hard to focus on it properly with all the interruptions- flattering interruptions though they were." He could easily see the stiffening of her neck and shoulders thanks to her upswept hairstyle.

"Flattering hmm?" She rolled her eyes. "Why Kraven? Because it just makes a black woman's day to have a white man tell her she's lovely?"

Kraven nodded. He'd guessed she was a woman who wore her looks with unease but hated to think it had anything to do with the reason she'd just shared.

He took a step forward. "Did that make you feel uncomfortable?"

"Did *what* make me feel uncomfortable?"

Kraven winced, but didn't lose his nerve. "Did someone offend you tonight?"

Darby turned her anger towards him then. Anger towards anyone was without merit. No one had actually offended her. Still, the anger stirred all the same and; as Kraven was its nearest recipient...

"Did anyone offend me?" She folded her arms across her chest and continued to brood toward the view. "You mean did anyone spout off one of the numerous stereotypical insights that white men think flatter black women? How our bodies look like they're made for fucking or how...enthusiastic we are in the sack?"

Kraven tasted bile souring the back of his throat and couldn't help but grimace. How many times had he been within earshot of conversations where those very words had been spoken? They angered him then and now that anger was compounded by the fact that the woman he'd come to treasure probably had those very words spoken to her.

"I pride myself on not being an idiot, Darby." He managed to keep the rage from coloring his voice and kept clenched fists shielded in his trouser pockets. "I also take pride in not having idiots for friends. If you were offended, then I am sorry."

She felt like a heel and didn't need to look his way to know she'd hurt him. His voice relayed it all just fine. She'd been prepared (and subconsciously anticipating) an offensive incident that night. She was disappointed and left with no where to direct her anger except toward him. He was the last person she wanted to quarrel with- the last person who deserved her anger. Yet she stood there warring with stubbornness until her phone vibrated inside the small purse on her shoulder. She dug it out and; seeing the name on the faceplate, all else fled her mind.

"What is it? What's wrong?" Darby's eyes were wide when she pressed the phone to her ear. "What? No..." she turned from the balcony and walked until she found the first chair to sink into. "When?...How?...yes, yes you know I will...no don't be stupid, you know I'll be there... alright... alright, bye."

"That was Nile," she explained feeling Kraven towering above her. "Her mother...her mother is dead." She felt his hand clutch her upper arm. "She- she was killed."

"How?" He whispered his emerald stare narrowed in suspicion and disbelief.

Darby was shaking her head. "You'll have to call Taurus. Nile...could hardly tell me anything." With effort, she pushed out of the chair. "Kraven I have to go." She waited for him to release her arm.

He didn't. "I can have you there in a few hours."

Again, she was shaking her head. "I need to go now. I-I need to go alone."

He released her then. His heart slowed, but he wouldn't question where things stood. She didn't need that then. Instead he calmed himself with the knowledge that she was his. It would just take more time. It would take time and a great deal of effort to get her to see the extent to which she'd possessed him. Asking him to walk away- to give up on what they might have just wasn't an option for him.

Darby accepted him releasing her arm as the end of the dramatic events for the evening. Awkwardly she inched around him. "I'll just get my stuff. We're in Edinburgh- it shouldn't be far to the airport, right?"

"A car will be waiting downstairs when you're ready to go." His voice was soft and it was a wonder he could remain standing as weak as he'd become. "What about the rest of your things?"

"I'll let you know where to send them." She sprinted up the stairway.

NINE

Los Angeles, California~ One Week Later...

Kraven pushed the fist; that had been poised to knock, back inside his jean pocket. He'd been telling himself that she needed more time but...patience had never been his strong suit.

Actually, he hadn't even given her a day. He'd headed out the very next morning after she'd left Edinburgh and followed her out to Seattle for Yvonne Wilson's funeral. The service was over when he arrived. He found Nile shaking hands with the few souls in attendance and went to offer his condolences.

He knew without asking that Darby was gone. Nile confirmed that he'd just missed her and the knowledge of that threatened to break him down right there. The newlyweds didn't begrudge him leaving. They knew his underlying reasons for attending the service.

Nile wished him luck and it was easy for Kraven to sense that there was more she wanted to say. He didn't need to hear it for he could very well imagine the ugly events that had shaped Darby Ellis' life and forced her to react to things the way she did.

Instead of a lecture, Nile only gave him the address and told him to be careful with her friend.

Kraven closed his eyes then and recalled his response to Nile's instruction: He loved Darby too much to be anything else.

Now, standing outside her door, he didn't have a devil of a clue as to how to proceed. He'd even put off going to see her for the first few days after his arrival. Finally he realized that coming up with the perfect approach would be impossible. The dilemma was taken out of his hands seconds later.

"Damn blood-sucking plumbers," Darby was growling when she pulled open her door. A cell phone was pressed to her ear while her other hand gripped a heavy portfolio case. "Shelby just tell him to keep his pants up and I'll-" she turned, words failing at the sight of Kraven DeBurgh filling her doorway.

"Tell him no more haggling- he doesn't like it we'll go someplace else." She shut down the phone and gazed upon Kraven in awe.

He acted as though an appearance in her doorway were an everyday occurrence. "In or out?" He asked, waving toward the portfolio.

Of course, Darby couldn't answer. She simply blinked and stepped back from the door. Kraven took the large square case and leaned it to a wall while kicking the door shut. Casually, he strolled in; taking in the surroundings of her home and smiling at its mellow elegance. The pastel coloring offset the brick walls and lent an almost tangible yet understated warmth to the dwelling.

Darby watched as he observed, unable to get over how at ease he appeared. In Scotland, she believed the man would look out of place anywhere other than his manor house with the castle eclipsing it. That image however was simply another facet to his allure. It was the cool that could only shawl the heat, the gentleness which shadowed the power.

Still, none of that prepared her for the element of defeat that clung to him when he appeared to give out and sink to her sofa. He leaned forward, head bowed, elbows braced on his knees.

On uncertain steps, Darby moved closer to one of the two armchairs that flanked the sofa. He began to speak just as her fingers clenched the back of the chair.

"I was about seventeen when I ran away. *Really* ran away." He clarified with a pitiful attempt at smirking. "There's a cluster of islands above Scotland- the Orkneys. Further out, there's another called Shetland Islands, but between those two are others- smaller...many aren't even charted." He dragged a hand through his hair and cleared his throat. "I made my way to the Orkneys looking for one of my uncles...I didn't find him, but what I did find..."

Darby was seated on the armchair by then, her legs tucked up and hidden beneath the pleats of her azure skirt. She was riveted and didn't even want to breathe for fear he'd stop talking.

"*Somehow*...I found my way to a boat that was headed toward the Shetlands. It was a boat filled with other kids- boys my age. They were all talking about some fantastic oasis that was waiting for them…I had no idea what the hell they meant, didn't dare call too much attention to myself as I was a mere stowaway…" he appeared to relax a bit as he purged more of the story. "The others had been educated, *sold* on the idea that whatever this place was it was a damn sight better than anything any of us had come from. It all sounded like heaven to me- getting away from my parents, responsibility, expectations, rules…I was all for it." His baritone voice wavered slightly. "It wasn't an oasis though…it was…" he couldn't finish, gave a jerky shrug to silence whatever else he'd been prepared to share.

He buried his face in his hands and shuddered. Darby tightened her grip on the seat cushions to stop herself from going to him.

"I've done things Darby. Things I've done out of a belief that they were for the best reasons- with the most honorable intentions. With age comes…clarity." He smiled then and finally looked over at her.

"Working my family's land now is as much about silencing my demons as it is about being redeemed for the actions I committed because of them." His shoulders rose beneath the black denim jacket he sported. "I've got a feeling the redemption part's gonna take a lot more effort than erecting a lodge and becoming a farmer."

Darby moved closer then. "Why are you doing this?" She brushed his hand from his hair and replaced it with her own. "Why would you belittle what you're trying to do to improve your life?"

Kraven was grabbing her hand before she even realized he'd moved. "Because I've done all this with no expectation of reward-no expectation of happiness. Ever. Then, there you were." His striking greens raked her face.

"I don't know whether God is torturing me- reminding me of one more thing I'd better not expect or whether there is a reward for my redemption."

"Kraven-"

"I love you."

"What?"

"Don't do that," he snapped and gave her hand a warning squeeze. "Don't act like you've got no idea. Did you really think this was just sex?" Sleek brows rose briefly. "Earth shattering as it is, it's a great deal more…for me anyway."

Her hand went limp inside his.

"I'm sorry for what happened in Scotland, Darby."

She scooted close then and rested her fingers across his mouth. "There's nothing for you to apologize for. Nothing." She blinked to keep pressuring tears at bay. "You showed me the best time, gave me nothing but your respect…your friends were only being nice- with lots of enthusiasm, but nothing more."

"No lass," his brows drew close and he cupped her face. "They weren't being *nice*. They were being bloody honest as hell."

Her smile was sweetness and sorrow intertwined. "You can't love me, Kraven. " She took note of the anger blazing in his eyes but scooter closer to him just the same. "Do you know what kind of agitation, frustration, sorrow, rage…you're letting yourself in for?" She shook her head. "I've experienced it so often that I'm weary of it. I wouldn't wish it on my worst enemy and I-"

He broke her speech with a lusty kiss that had her moaning seconds after his tongue had engaged hers.

"Kraven stop," she resisted until he allowed her to push him away barely. "Do you think your friends would

be flattering if they knew your feelings went deeper than
lust for a little weekend diversion? Or what about the good
people in that beautiful little town of yours? Do you really
think they'd accept this? And these...these sons you speak
of having- with *me*? Please! Do you actually think your
family would accept your black sons Kraven?"

"Yes, love."

His answer was so endearing and given without a
second of hesitation. Her heart melted along with the rest of
her and she could only slump back on the sofa. She was
stunned and could think of nothing else to say. He knelt
before her, the beautiful scarred hands curled around the
backs of her knees.

"I canna begin to understand all the hurt and ugly
things you've had to endure, love." He bowed his head,
nuzzling the crook of her neck. "I hope that in time I can
fill your world with things as incredible as you are-things
that'll push all that ugliness to a place in your mind that
you'll never have to revisit."

The tears wouldn't remain at bay then. They filled
the shamrock green of her stare and blurred the intensity of
Kraven's when he moved back to study her. Quickly she
wiped the wetness from her cheeks.

"I've experienced this *ugliness* at both ends, you
know?" She sat a little straighter on the sofa. "I've had the
misfortune of attaching my emotions to black men I was
too white for and white men I was too black for. It never
worked out with any of them," her smile was sad and
trembled in the wake of a sob. "Do you know what that
does to a person after while Kraven? Can you imagine what
it does to a woman?"

He leaned close again, pressing his forehead to hers. "Were any of them- any of those men…were any of them me, lass?"

She cried then, unabashed and unrelenting. The tears splashed to the hands clenched in her lap. Kraven let her expel the emotion, knowing it'd most likely been pent up for years. He moved to the sofa, pulling her flush against him.

"Hold onto me, lass." He kissed her cheek, "Hold onto me. If you believe in me, what I can give you, what you can give me, hold onto me."

She clutched him then, desperate for him, desiring him, loving him…

"It's alright, it's alright," he soothed, smiling as he rocked her.

For the first time in her life, Darby believed it was true.

His mouth began a slow graze at her temple, along the curve of her cheekbone and he laughed when she spoke the words he longed to hear.

"Kraven, Kraven I do love you. I love you." She professed moments before his kiss claimed her and she repeated the words when he finally let her up for air.

The kiss went from sweet and promising, to branding and fiery in the span of seconds. That familiar elation Kraven felt with Darby in his arms surged up and throughout. It filled him with a euphoria that he could (and would) live on forever.

Darby bit her lip when he broke the kiss to ravage her neck with the scrape of his perfect teeth and seductive mouth.

"Where shall I take you?"

She heard him speaking against her ear and her heart jerked. God, was this man really here? Really hers? She didn't know what tomorrow or the tomorrows after that would bring, but he'd found the part of her she'd sworn closed forever and he felt right. He felt oh so very right there.

"Darby?"

She heard him call when she offered no answer to his question. Nuzzling her nose with his, she coaxed him into another kiss.

They settled to the center of her bed in a tangle of arms and legs. Midday sunlight fought to stream through closed blinds. Golden rays streaked the violet walls and coordinating fabrics of the furniture and bed linens. Darby's helpless sounds of need and arousal were challenged by the sounds of his.

She buried her fingers in the lush blackness of his hair, the same way his hid in her riot of honey blonde curls and massaged her scalp. The sweetness of the moment was treasured, but Darby wanted more and she told him so.

Kraven shuddered when her words touched his ears. She didn't have to tell him twice. In moments, his hands were quickly, expertly relieving her of the flippy skirt, matching top and under things. He kissed and suckled every part of her bared to his stare.

Darby's breathing came in gasping waves. She was overwhelmed, aroused and just a tad unsettled by his hunger. She welcomed every bit of it though, and wasn't about to be outdone. With the same ferocity, she tugged him from his clothes, worshipping his chiseled bronzed frame with her kisses, her gaze, her touch...

"Don't wait," she ordered when they were both nude and clinging amidst the rumpled bed coverings.

One swift plunge buried him inside her. His eyes were riveted on her face, searching for any signs of discomfort. There were none, only a basic hunger filtered her vibrant stare and reflected the emotion in his.

"More," she encouraged, raking her nails along his back. Her hands moved down to clutch his butt nestled half in, half out of the sheets as he stroked her with a slow seductive rhythm that had her crying out for him in some undecipherable language.

Kraven draped one of her legs across his shoulder, increasing the depth of his already magnificent thrusting power. Darby's resulting moan came out on a breathless laugh of utter bliss. Kraven dipped his head to her shoulder when he felt her increased moisture soak his shaft.

He muttered a lurid curse while clutching the bed linens in one hand and her thigh in the other. His movements inside her gained speed and fire while he chanted her name. He burrowed his handsome face deeper into her neck to inhale her scent- her essence.

Darby laid clenching and unclenching the pillows cluttering the headboard. She bit her lip and threatened to draw blood at the sensation of his release oozing warm and heavy inside her. The feel of it had her orgasmic again in the span of a millisecond.

They rocked upon each other in a dance of mutual desire. Once the potent throbs of want began to ebb, they continued to rock until a powerful wave of sleep claimed them both.

Kraven roused from his slumber and found himself still intimately connected to the woman he loved. He smiled, knowing the gesture was echoed in his heart. His smiled deepened then and he gave a quick shake of his head. His heart had never been anything other than the organ to pump the blood that kept him alive. Now, it pumped with the force of blood *and* love and he realized for the first time that he was and felt truly alive.

Kissing the relaxed curve of her mouth, he slowly withdrew and winced as renewed desire for her stirred his shaft.

Darby's lashes fluttered when she emerged just slightly from her sleep. She appeared cozy and her smile was content at the sight of him looming near.

"Are you okay?" She asked, studying his darkly lovely face in wonder.

"Are you?" He countered, his mouth twisting somewhat ruefully. "I apologize for falling asleep... inside...Jesus," he moaned as the sounds of the words stiffened his sex.

"Never apologize for that," she whispered and raked his hair back from his forehead. "Are you coming back?"

Kraven groaned as if tortured. "I fully intend to as soon as I get something on my stomach."

"Ah, we've proven it then," Darby chuckled sleepily. "Love is no substitute for food."

"What can I say, sweet? I'm Scottish." He leaned in to help himself to a kiss that turned sultry in a second.

Darby broke the kiss and pressed another to his ear. "Kitchen's on the other side of the living room."

"I'll be back," he growled into her chest.

Darby was already drifting back to sleep. "'Kay," she murmured.

Kraven nuzzled his face in her hair and inhaled. "I love you."

"I love you back..."

The serenity and assurance in that single phrase had him grinning like a kid. Shaking his head, he softly ordered himself from the bed and followed her directions to the kitchen. He settled on a can of soup, figuring that'd take the edge off until he took Darby out for dinner later.

While waiting on the microwave to heat the soup, he grabbed bottled water from the fridge and took a tour of the condo. He felt relaxed by the pastel color scheme, the view, even the pieces adorning the walls.

The microwave beeped but Kraven was too entranced by the art which any gallery owner would be thrilled to have. His gaze narrowed when he glimpsed the piece hanging in a tiny alcove.

The water bottle slid from his hand.

As though led by some invisible thread, Kraven moved in for a closer look. When full realization settled in, his heart could've taken the same plunge the bottle had.

Blindly, he stumbled from the alcove in search of his jacket which he found draped across the back of the sofa. He reached for his phone and dialed absently.

"Hill? Kraven. Remember what you said about the tide turning? I believe it's about to."

EPILOGUE

Monterrey, California~ Two weeks later...

Darby pressed her lips together to keep from laughing when Kraven dropped down beside her on the front porch swing that faced the gorgeous strip of beach across the street.

"Mama thinks you're very sweet and...oh what else did she say? Oh! Sexy as hell," she chuckled then before slanting him a glance. "Sorry about my dad. He doesn't mean to be so intimidating it's the whole military thing."

Kraven nodded watching his sneaker shod foot perched on the porch railing. "There's that and then I just had to add to the need for intimidation by asking for his daughter's hand in marriage."

87

Darby's recline in the swing ended and she bolted straight. "His daughter's... what?!"

"Hand-in-marriage," Kraven replied with deliberate slowness. "It's when the groom-to-be goes to the lady's father and-"

Darby slapped his arm. "I know what it is, dammit."

"Ah! Good, then you know what comes next." He reached into the pocket of his jeans.

Darby stood from the swing when she saw the small cream velvet box. "Kraven-" her voice resembled a frog's croak and; embarrassed, she grimaced. "Kraven-"

"Right," he moved off the swing as well but knelt before her instead of standing. "Be my wife please. I promise you'll not be sorry."

She had to smile even as precautions tickled her throat. She had to share them.

"Are you sure Kraven? This is happening so fast."

"Just like everything else that's happened between us. Why stop now?"

She shook her head. "Are you sure?"

He stood then. "More than I've ever been about anything else in my entire life." His gaze lowered. "Do you want me Darby?"

She smoothed the back of her hand across his cheek. "More than I've ever wanted anything else in *my* entire life."

They merged into a kiss and Kraven eased the ring onto her finger. "May I have my answer now?" He asked while his tongue played with hers.

She merely deepened the kiss.

"Is that a yes?" He grinned.

"That is most definitely a yes, Lord DeBurgh."

He pulled back before she could kiss him again. "Once we're married, you'll only be allowed to use that name in the privacy of our bedroom when we're doing the most enjoyable things."

"Mmm…" she shivered when his mouth teased her earlobe. "So you're saying I'll be using it quite often, then?"

"Oh yes, Ms. Ellis. Oh yes…"

Dear Reader,

I hope you'll agree that Kraven & Darby needed to have their story told. So often, authors are asked whether they'll create stories for the various secondary characters whose roles are required for the progression of the story. Many times those characters go no farther than the main story. Other times, the characters are so riveting they demand no less than their own title.

Lover's Allure is one of those titles. I hope I've succeeded in bringing to life the heat and emotion that practically surges to life between Kraven DeBurgh & Darby Ellis. This being my first interracial love story, I hope it met your expectations.

There will be more of Kraven & Darby. For now, please know that your support and motivation are very treasured.

Let me know what you think:
altonya@lovealtonya.com

Blessings & Love,
AlTonya
www.lovealtonya.com

An AlTonya Exclusive

www.ingramcontent.com/pod-product-compliance
Lightning Source LLC
Chambersburg PA
CBHW031857170626
46807CB00004B/1768